CANADA

Newfoundland
and Labrador

Prince
Edward
Island

Quebec

Nova
Scotia

Ontario

New Brunswick

A Day in Canada

Per-Henrik Gürth

Kids Can Press

Bbbbrrring! It's time to wake up.
What will you do today?

7:15 a.m.

Help unload fresh vegetables at the Halifax Farmers' Market.

5:15 p.m.
Trek through the treetops near Whistler Mountain.

Barbecue on the beach
at Great Slave Lake.

What a fun day!
What time do you like to ...

For Emily and Ben

The Inuktitut word in the story is
Sinittiarniaqputit *(See-NEET-tee-A-nee-A-poo-TEET)*: Goodnight

Text © 2015 Kids Can Press
Illustrations © 2015 Per-Henrik Gürth

Kids Can Press acknowledges the financial support of the Government of Ontario, through the Ontario Media Development Corporation's Ontario Book Initiative; the Ontario Arts Council; the Canada Council for the Arts; and the Government of Canada, through the CBF, for our publishing activity.

Published in Canada by   Published in the U.S. by
Kids Can Press Ltd.   Kids Can Press Ltd.
25 Dockside Drive   2250 Military Road
Toronto, ON M5A 0B5   Tonawanda, NY 14150

www.kidscanpress.com

The artwork in this book was rendered in Adobe Illustrator.
The text is set in Province Sans Bold.

Edited by Katie Scott
Designed by Julia Naimska

This book is smyth sewn casebound.
Manufactured in Tseung Kwan O, NT Hong Kong, China, in 11/2014 by Paramount Printing Co. Ltd.

CM 15 0 9 8 7 6 5 4 3 2 1

Library and Archives Canada Cataloguing in Publication

Gürth, Per-Henrik, author, illustrator
    A day in Canada / written and illustrated by Per-Henrik Gürth.

ISBN 978-1-77138-125-3 (bound)

    1. Canada — Juvenile literature. I. Title.

FC76.G87 2015   j971   C2014-902624-2

Kids Can Press is a *l*©**r**u**s**™ Entertainment company